WHEN HAL DAVID AND I WROTE THIS SONG IN 1965,
IT WAS AN OBSERVATION ON WHAT WAS GOING ON IN
THE WORLD, AND WE THOUGHT IT WAS AN IMPORTANT
STATEMENT TO MAKE. NOW, DECADES LATER, THE SONG'S
MEANING HAS BECOME MUCH MORE POWERFUL. WE'RE
SO GLAD WE WROTE THIS SONG, AND ARE DELIGHTED
THAT YOU CAN NOW ENJOY IT AS A BOOK.

— BURT BACHARACH

♥　♥　♥　♥　♥

PENGUIN WORKSHOP

Penguin Young Readers Group
An Imprint of Penguin Random House LLC

"What the World Needs Now Is Love Sweet Love"
Words and Music by Hal David and Burt Bacharach
© 1965 (Renewed 1993) BMG Rights Management (UK) Ltd. (PRS) /
Songs Of Fujimusic (PRS) / New Hidden Valley Music Co. (ASCAP)
All Rights Adm. by BMG Rights Management (US) LLC.
Used By Permission. All Rights Reserved.

Illustrations copyright © 2017 by Mary Kate McDevitt.
All rights reserved. Published by Penguin Workshop, an imprint of Penguin Random House LLC,
345 Hudson Street, New York, New York 10014. PENGUIN and PENGUIN WORKSHOP are
trademarks of Penguin Books Ltd, and the W colophon is a trademark of Penguin Random House LLC.
Manufactured in China.

Library of Congress Cataloging-in-Publication Data is available.

ISBN 9781524785987 　　10 9 8 7 6 5 4 3 2 1

WHAT THE WORLD NEEDS NOW IS LOVE

WRITTEN BY
BURT BACHARACH and **HAL DAVID**
ILLUSTRATED by MARY KATE McDEVITT

PENGUIN WORKSHOP ♥ AN IMPRINT of PENGUIN RANDOM HOUSE

WHAT the
NEEDS
L♥VE,

It's the only thing that

What the world needs now is LOVE, sweet LOVE. NO, NOT JUST FOR SOME, BUT FOR Everyone.

Lord, we don't need another mountain.

There are MOUNTAINS and HILLSIDES enough to CLIMB.

There are OCEANS and Rivers ENOUGH to CROSS,

ENOUGH to LAST till the END of TIME.

WHAT the WORLD NEEDS NOW IS LOVE, SWEET LOVE.

IT'S the ONLY
THING
THAT THERE'S
JUST TOO
LITTLE
of.

NO, NOT JUST FOR SOME, BUT FOR EVERYONE.

THERE ARE CORN FIELDS AND WHEAT FIELDS ENOUGH TO GROW.

There are **SUNBEAMS** and

WHAT THE WORLD needs now is LOVE, SWEET LOVE.

WHAT the NEEDS LOVE,

EVERY, EVERY, Everyone.

WHAT the WORLD NEEDS

NOW is LOVE, sweet LOVE.